# Dear Parent:

Congratulations! Your child is taking the first steps on an exciting journey. The destination? Independent reading!

**STEP INTO READING®** will help your child get there. The program offers five steps to reading success. Each step includes fun stories and colorful art. There are also Step into Reading Sticker Books, Step into Reading Math Readers, Step into Reading Write-In Readers, Step into Reading Phonics Readers, and Step into Reading Phonics First Steps! Boxed Sets—a complete literacy program with something for every child.

## Learning to Read, Step by Step!

**Ready to Read** **Preschool–Kindergarten**
• big type and easy words • rhyme and rhythm • picture clues
For children who know the alphabet and are eager to begin reading.

**Reading with Help** **Preschool–Grade 1**
• basic vocabulary • short sentences • simple stories
For children who recognize familiar words and sound out new words with help.

**Reading on Your Own** **Grades 1–3**
• engaging characters • easy-to-follow plots • popular topics
For children who are ready to read on their own.

**Reading Paragraphs** **Grades 2–3**
• challenging vocabulary • short paragraphs • exciting stories
For newly independent readers who read simple sentences with confidence.

**Ready for Chapters** **Grades 2–4**
• chapters • longer paragraphs • full-color art
For children who want to take the plunge into chapter books but still like colorful pictures.

**STEP INTO READING®** is designed to give every child a successful reading experience. The grade levels are only guides. Children can progress through the steps at their own speed, developing confidence in their reading, no matter what their grade.

Remember, a lifetime love of reading starts with a single step!

*For Andrew, Shelby, Anna, Max, and Lucy*
*—A.J.H.*

*To Elaine*
*—H.W.S.*

Text copyright © 2010 by Anna Jane Hays
Illustrations copyright © 2010 by Hala Wittwer Swearingen

Visit us on the Web!
www.stepintoreading.com

Educators and librarians, for a variety of teaching tools, visit us at
www.randomhouse.com/teachers

*Library of Congress Cataloging-in-Publication Data*
Hays, Anna Jane.
Spring surprises / by Anna Jane Hays ; illustrated by Hala Wittwer Swearingen.
    p. cm. — (Step into reading. Step 2 book)
Summary: A rhyming tribute to the wonders brought by spring.
ISBN 978-0-375-85840-6 (trade pbk.) — ISBN 978-0-375-95840-3 (lib. bdg.)
[1. Stories in rhyme. 2. Spring—Fiction.] I. Swearingen, Hala Wittwer, ill. II. Title.
PZ8.3.H3337Sp 2010
[E]—dc22 2009013383

Printed in the United States of America

10 9 8 7 6 5 4 3 2 1

# Spring Surprises

by Anna Jane Hays

illustrated by Hala Wittwer Swearingen

Random House ⌂ New York

Wake up, wake up!
Spring is here,
calling us outside.
Frosty winter,
say goodbye!

Hello, blue sky,
where birds fly high
and clouds puff by.

The groundhog has
come up to stay.

The bear cub has
come out to play.

Welcome, sunshine,
warm our cheeks.
Melt the snow and
fill the creeks.

Welcome, wind,
come fly our kites!

Greet longer days
and shorter nights.

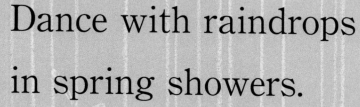

Dance with raindrops
in spring showers.

Watch buds open
into flowers.

Come discover
spring's surprises.

Pick and smell
the pretty prizes.

Make mud pies
to bake on rocks.

Make dollies
out of hollyhocks.

In the pond,
count pollywogs.
Watch them all
turn into frogs.

See the duckling
learn to swim.
Mother duck
is proud of him.

Look up, look up!

What's in the nest?

Climb up and peek.

Hop like bunnies,

hide and seek.

Robins bathe
in a puddle.
Little mouse
has to scuttle!

Hello,
yellow baby chicks,
calf that licks,
kid that kicks.

Welcome,
woolly little lamb.
You all are part of
spring's grand plan.

The sun stays up
so we can play
until late in
this spring day.

When stars pop out
in the night sky,
spring sings a loving
lullaby.

Bullfrogs croak,
owls *WHO-WHO*.
That is all
this day can do.

Now  and I need

**BABY JAGUAR**

to get warm and dry too!

Thanks for helping!

We helped the 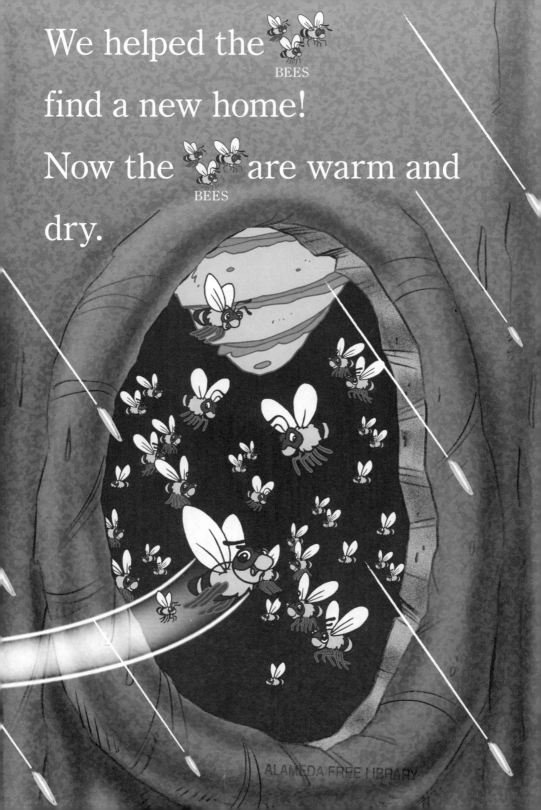 BEES
find a new home!
Now the BEES are warm and
dry.

The  are going
inside the 🌳.
TREE
The 🐝🐝 are safe!
BEES

We will hold the
UMBRELLA

over the .
BEES

Now we need to show the
BEES

the way to the .
TREE

What can we use
to protect the ? BEES

An ☂! UMBRELLA

Good job!

The  has started!
RAIN

We need to protect the 🐝🐝
BEES

from the ☁️ .
RAIN

🎒 can help us
RESCUE PACK

protect the 🐝🐝 !
BEES

This  is a great place

TREE

for a 🪺 !

HIVE

It has a big ⬡

HOLE

and no one else lives here.

The 🐝🐝 can live here!

BEES

What about this ?
TREE

It has a big ⬡.
HOLE

We need to look inside

the ⬡.
HOLE

The ⬡ is empty!
HOLE

This  has a big ⬡.
ROCK WALL · HOLE

But a 🕷 lives here.
SPIDER

The  will keep the 🕷
ROCK WALL · SPIDER

dry.

We have to keep looking

for a ⬡ for the 🐝.
HOLE · BEES

This 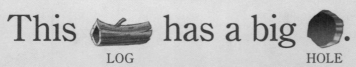 has a big ⬡.
LOG                                    HOLE
But a 🐍 lives here.
SNAKE
The 🪵 will keep the 🐍 dry.
LOG                              SNAKE
We have to keep looking

for a ⬡ for the 🐝.
HOLE                    BEES

Quick!

The  is almost here!

RAIN

The  BEES say they need a big HOLE for their HIVE. We need to find a place with a big HOLE.

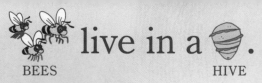 live in a ⬡.

BEES            HIVE

Help us find a good place

for a new ⬡!

HIVE

The 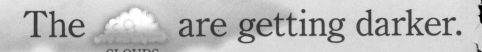 are getting darker.
CLOUDS

We need to hurry!

Do not worry, !
BEES

We will help you find

a new home!

Do you see the  ?
BEES
There they are!

Do you see the big  ?
ROCK

There it is!

The BEES are near

the big ROCK .

The  **BEES** need to find a new home before the **RAIN** starts. **BEES** cannot fly in heavy **RAIN**. To the rescue!

  found a group of  .

BEES

CLICK THE CAMERA

I hear a buzzing sound.

An animal is in trouble!

What animal is it?

 can help!

CLICK THE CAMERA

Quick!

We need to close the  .
WINDOW

We can stay dry inside.

Hi! I am  .
DIEGO

This is  .
BABY JAGUAR

Do you see dark  ?
CLOUDS

It looks like it will  .
RAIN

Based on the TV series *Go, Diego, Go!*™ as seen on Nick Jr.®

SIMON SPOTLIGHT

An imprint of Simon & Schuster Children's Publishing Division

1230 Avenue of the Americas, New York, New York 10020

Manufactured in the United States of America

First Edition

2 4 6 8 10 9 7 5 3 1

Library of Congress Cataloging-in-Publication Data

Inches, Alison.

Diego's buzzing bee adventure / by Alison Inches ; illustrated by Ron Zalme. —1st ed.

p. cm. — (Ready-to-Read)

"Based on the TV series Go, Diego, Go!(tm) as seen on Nick Jr."

ISBN-13: 978-1-4169-4776-9

ISBN-10: 1-4169-4776-0

I. Zalme, Ron. II. Go, Diego, go! (Television program) III. Title.

PZ7.I355Dhm 2008

2007006614

# Diego's Buzzing Bee Adventure

by Alison Inches

illustrated by Ron Zalme

Ready-to-Read

Simon Spotlight/Nick Jr.
New York   London   Toronto   Sydney